Bimmi Finds a Cat

Bimmi Finds a Cat

by Elisabeth J. Stewart

Illustrated by James E. Ransome

Clarion Books/*New York*

Clarion Books
a Houghton Mifflin Company imprint
215 Park Avenue South, New York, NY 10003
Text copyright © 1996 by Elisabeth J. Stewart
Illustrations copyright © 1996 by James E. Ransome

The illustrations for this book were executed in oil paints on watercolor paper.
The text was set in 13/17.5 pt. Palatino.

Printed in the USA

Library of Congress Cataloging-in-Publication Data

Stewart, Elisabeth Jane.
Bimmi finds a cat / by Elisabeth J. Stewart ; illustrated by James E. Ransome.
p.   cm.
Summary: An eight-year-old Creole boy on Galveston Island grieves
the death of his cat Crabmeat, but when another lost cat leads him
to a new friend he starts to heal.
ISBN 0-395-64652-9
[1. Cats—Fiction. 2. Lost and found possessions—Fiction. 3. Death—Fiction.
4. Grief—Fiction. 5. Creoles—Fiction. 6. Galveston Island (Tex.)—Fiction.]
I. Ransome, James E., ill.   II. Title.
PZ7.S848795Bi   1996
[Fic]—dc20   94-12780
                                              CIP
                                              AC

BVG 10 9 8 7 6 5 4 3 2 1

Dedicated to all the children who have ever lost a pet
and also to my husband, Ben,
who is kind to little mice.
E.J.S.

To Tom Feelings—
thanks for your wisdom.
J.E.R.

Chapter 1

Bimmi Ladouce ran along the fishing pier looking for his cat, Crabmeat. The Gulf of Mexico off Galveston Island was fairly calm this morning, so the brown planks were warm and dry underfoot. He looked under nets hung to dry, behind casks by the fishing supply shacks, under an overturned boat. But there was no Crabmeat, no slinky gray cat with his rib bones showing.

Crabmeat ate a lot, but not enough to get fat like some cats. He ran it all off at night, Mama said.

Just as he was thinking about Mama, Bimmi heard her calling from their shack on the edge of the beach. "Bimmi! Bimmi, where you at?"

I'll go back as soon as I find my cat, Bimmi promised silently. He felt worried. Crabmeat never came down here before Bimmi did. The cat would come in from his night's playing, stretch and yawn, then sleep at the foot of Bimmi's mat until Bimmi got up. But he wasn't there this morning.

Little waves winked and foamed around the pilings under the pier. When Bimmi looked down, he saw seaweed in the water, shells at the bottom, and the shadow of a fish now and then. He wished he had brought his fishing rod with him. He sat on the outer edge of the last plank, wondering where Crabmeat might be.

"Bimmi!" There was Mama's voice again. "Bimmi, come eat your breakfast. Come on now, hear?"

Bimmi was hungry, for sure. He unfolded his legs, stood up, and plodded back up the pier toward home.

He climbed up the pole ladder into the shack. Mama, bright and pretty in her flowered dress and her yellow head rag, smiled at him and gave him a plate of cornbread and fried fish.

"*Merci*, Mama," Bimmi said politely. "Mama, you see Crabmeat anywhere? I been looking for him, and he not here, not there, nowhere at all. Me, I'm worried about him." He bit into the cornbread.

Mama shook her head. "He probably chasing little girl cat somewhere, or chasing bird, one. Maybe go up into cottages, forget to come home, yes? You eat and then go look. Or maybe he be back by time you finish food."

Bimmi ate his breakfast, but because he was worried, it didn't taste as good as usual. He made himself think about something besides his missing cat.

"Where P'pa, Mama?" he asked. "He not get in last night, him? Other shrimpers, they back, some of them."

"He came, yes, but he gone out again. He be back tonight, *peut-être*, perhaps."

Breakfast was finished, but Crabmeat hadn't appeared. Bimmi got up, kissed Mama, and went flying down the ladder. The cottages? That was a good idea. *Someone up there maybe feeding that little devil cat*, he thought. *Crabmeat always want food.*

Bimmi started up the road. Sunlight shimmered on the white surface, which was made of crushed oyster shells.

The road ran through a grove of coconut palms. Bimmi saw a small gray shape in the shadow of one tree, lying very still. He wandered toward it, carefully not looking at it. That was what Crabmeat always did when he wanted to pretend he wasn't interested in something.

Finally Bimmi looked down at the small gray shape at his feet. Suddenly tears were flowing down his cheeks. It was Crabmeat, all right. No telling what had happened to him, but there was no sign of a fight, no blood, nothing to say, "This is how a brave cat died."

Bimmi bent down and gathered his cat into his arms. He turned and walked slowly back home.

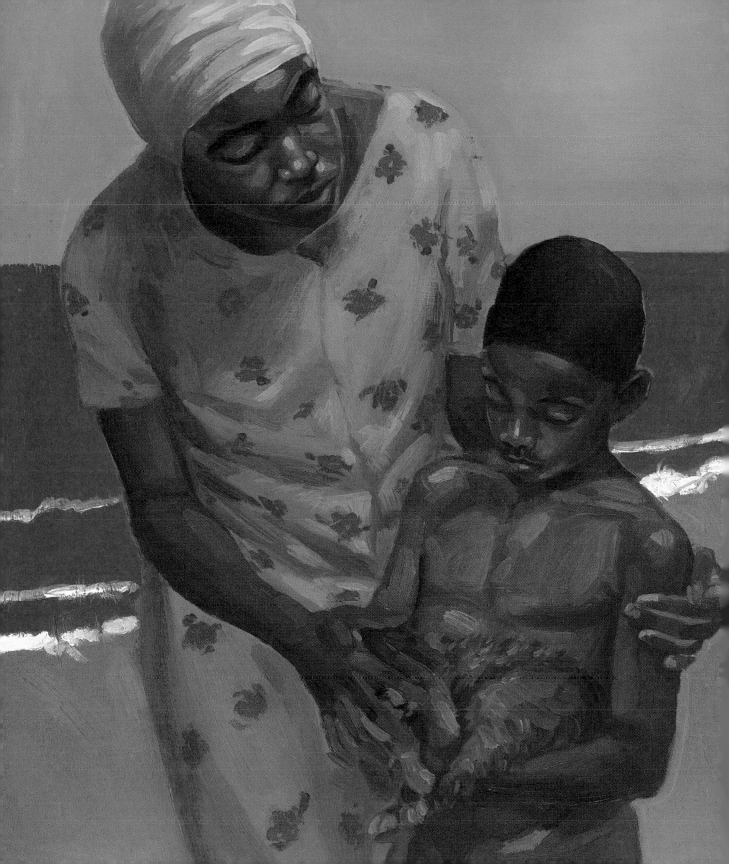

Chapter 2

Mama came down the ladder to meet him.

"Ah, Bimmi, how sad!" she said in a low voice. "Your cat, he gone to cat heaven now. Me, I'm so sorry, son. Here, give cat to me. I take care of him for you."

"No, Mama, *merci beaucoup*, but I take care of Crabmeat my own self," Bimmi said through his tears. "You come too?"

Mama helped him dig a grave high up on a dune in a patch of sand grass. She found a wooden shrimp box to put the cat in. Bimmi laid a pink shell between his cat's paws and covered him up good with strips of palm fronds. He shut the lid. Then he pushed the loose sand back over the box and pulled a log of driftwood over the little grave.

Bimmi wiped his eyes and turned to Mama. "Mama, you make a sign for me, write on a board, what a good cat Crabmeat was?"

Mama nodded. "I do that, son. I got washing to do now for Mrs. Dunbar. You go with your crab net and catch me some crab to sell, some crab to eat, before lunch time. I fix good crab gumbo, me, for when your papa come home tonight."

Bimmi went slowly back up the oyster-shell road to the tiny village called Pointe des Fleurs, passing the little gray frame schoolhouse where he and the eight other children of the shanty town went to school when a teacher was available. He had two thoughts in his mind. One was that he would fish from the pier that the people in the village used, instead of the rough one where Crabmeat had always kept him company. Usually he stayed away from the villagers. They had always been kind to him, and yet . . . they were like people from another world.

The other thought was that he would never enjoy his life again now that his cat was gone.

He brushed tears away fiercely. He would *not* be a cry-baby. But not crying didn't seem right either, somehow.

Bimmi stopped walking. He sat down beside the road and let pictures of Crabmeat come into his mind, and he cried freely. *Oh, cat,* he thought, *come back. I miss you.*

Chapter 3

A little sound came from behind him. "Mrrrrow?"

Bimmi whirled around, breathless. A cat? Crabmeat come back in answer to his plea?

It was a cat, all right, but not Crabmeat. This was a small dainty cat, a long-furred cat with orange and black and white patches all over, curious green eyes, and a waving plume of a tail. She came and nuzzled his knee, sniffing quietly at him. He patted her shyly, murmured little meows at her, and then took her in his lap.

"You lost, kitty?" he said, making his voice low like Mama's. "You don't belong no one, maybe? You hungry?"

The cat purred and bumped Bimmi's hand with her nose.

"You come with me, kitty, I feed you, me," said Bimmi. "I call you Kitty-Louise." He stood up, took his pole and crab net in one hand and the cat on the other arm, and walked slowly toward the village folks' pier.

He stepped slowly and carefully onto the white metal public pier, ducking his head and smiling shyly at the few men leaning on the railings, poles in their hands. The men smiled back at him. Bimmi didn't recognize any of them. He knew only a few of the summer people who stayed in the rental cottages. They came and they went. He knew two or three who lived all year round in the tiny village in the palms, half a mile from the real city of Galveston, but none of them seemed to be out on the pier today.

Bimmi tied a dead fish in the center of the crab net and lowered the net on its long rope to the bottom under the pier. Then he tended to his short pole with its cord line and heavy surf weights. *I get food for Mama to cook. She need me,* he thought proudly as he baited his hook. *Besides, I need some food for this Kitty-Louise.*

By sun-high he had two fat red snappers and ten crabs tied well with strands of kelp lying on the pier beside him, and Kitty-Louise was contentedly eating a small fish he had taken fresh from a crab's claws.

"Kitty-Louise, you eat all that lunch now, hear?" he said happily. "You eating for two, kitty. For you and for Crabmeat. He can't eat no more himself for himself. You eat. You stay a fat little cat."

Saying that, he looked carefully at his new cat. She was no starved cat. *This cat, she been eating good,* he told himself, and the thought awoke a little fear inside him. This cat had folks, she did. If she was lost, she hadn't been lost for long.

Bimmi sighed a deep sigh that hurt clear down to his toes. He couldn't just keep this Kitty-Louise. He had to find out whether she belonged to someone in the village.

At least none of the men on the pier had seemed to recognize her. That was a relief.

Bimmi carried the little cat home to show Mama. He gave Mama the fish and the string of kelp-and-crabs. She praised him, put the crabs into a tin basin, and admired the cat, who stretched out a paw and purred at her.

"Mama," Bimmi said, "this kitty, she too fat to be lost." He stopped and swallowed hard. "She—Mama, I think maybe she belong to someone. Whoever own her, miss her like I miss Crabmeat. Maybe I better find out."

Between bites of his lunch, Bimmi petted the cat, who was lying at his feet playing with a cowrie shell. When he was finished eating, Mama said, "She beautiful, Bimmi, and you perfectly right that you must find who own her."

Bimmi knew what he had to do, but did he have to do it right now? He hunted in his mind for a way to keep Kitty-Louise a little longer. If she stayed for a day or two, maybe she would want to stay for always.

"Mama, maybe she belong to some folks you do washing for," he said. "Maybe you ask them, when you take washing back to them? Tomorrow, next day?"

Mama didn't answer. She just smiled at him, and he understood. *It be my job to do,* he admitted to himself. *I do it, me.* He picked up the cat.

"You go back now, and don't be too long," said Mama. "You come home before supper, son." Mama waved at him as he set off once more on the white oyster-shell road.

Chapter 4

Bimmi was very tired, and the soles of his bare feet hurt a little from the sharp shells, by the time he had asked at three or four cottages whether someone there had lost this cat. But he was beginning to have hope. No one so far had claimed the cat. Kitty-Louise was still his. "Right of salvage," he murmured. Things washed up by the Gulf of Mexico onto Galveston Island were salvage, and whoever found them could keep them. Salvage helped the shrimp people live.

Sometimes usable boards were washed up. They went into the making of a little shed or an extra room for a shanty. Bimmi himself was trying to collect enough boards to make a room of his own.

No one ever stole another person's salvage. In fact, as far as Bimmi knew, no one in the tiny shanty town ever stole anything. People were too busy working; also, they had respect for one another, and for themselves.

"Kitty-Louise, you still salvage," he murmured lovingly to his little cat. She was almost asleep on his shoulder, like a many-colored fur shawl.

He stopped to talk with the few people he knew, people who gave his mama washing to do.

"I think I've seen that cat," one woman said from her tiny porch near the fence. "But I can't remember where."

"*Merci*, ma'am," Bimmi said, and went on.

In front of a small yellow cottage with green shutters, a gray-haired woman was weeding in her garden. She looked up as Bimmi knocked on the top of her gate.

"Yes? Can I help you—Oh, Patty Cake! You foolish cat, where have you been? I was looking for you!" She laid down her tools and held out her arms.

Bimmi pushed the gate open. The three-colored cat leaped lightly from his arms and ran to the woman, who picked up and cuddled her affectionately before setting her down again.

Bimmi's heart sank down to his toes. No more Kitty-Louise. He just could not win. Crabmeat gone this morning, and now Kitty-Louise was called Patty Cake and belonged to someone else. He started to turn away.

"No, no, young man," the woman said crisply. "You brought my cat home—I want to give you a reward. What would you like? Money? Cake, candy?"

Bimmi shook his head. "No ma'am, *merci beaucoup*, I don't need a thing. Glad to bring you your cat."

Now that was a lie, and he knew it, but it seemed like a good thing to say. He turned back toward the road.

"No, I mean it, really," the woman said. "I want to make you feel better. You look very sad. You liked this cat, didn't you? You didn't really want to bring her home to me."

Bimmi nodded. He knew he should pretend not to care, so that the woman could feel good about her cat instead of worrying about him. Even though he knew he had lost Kitty-Louise forever, he held his head up high.

"That be all right," he said to the woman, over the lump in his throat. "I know how it is to lose a cat, me." He looked down at Kitty-Louise, who came over to him and rubbed against his legs. He bent over to pet her, then drew his hand back.

"I tell you what, young man," the woman said suddenly. "This cat, she likes you. She gets bored, living with an old woman like me. And you look like a strong, dependable young man. If I'm going to live here on the island for good, I'm going to need someone to help me sometimes."

Bimmi felt a surge of hope. "Yes ma'am." What was she going to ask him to do? *I do it, no matter what,* he thought eagerly.

"My name is Mrs. Finch," she told him. "How about this—you come by here whenever you want, and take Patty Cake crabbing or fishing with you. That way she can be yours part of the time, and she won't go running off from me. I won't worry, because there will be two of us looking out for her. And sometimes you can keep me company too, and do little jobs for me. Like weeding and painting. Why don't you sit here with Patty Cake and think about it? I'll be right back." She turned and went into the cottage.

Bimmi sat on the ground and took the little cat in his lap. All his up-and-down feelings since this morning—worry over Crabmeat, grief at Crabmeat's death, delight at finding Kitty-Louise, and fear that he'd have to give her up—had worn him out. He could feel his heart pounding as if he had just run all the way from home. But he was happy.

"I come play with you every day, Kitty-Louise," he told the cat. "The rest of the time you be Patty Cake. Mrs. Finch, she give you plenty to eat. Me and Mrs. Finch, we take good care of you."

He stroked the cat and felt her purring. He felt like purring too.

Mrs. Finch came back outside with some cookies in a paper napkin. Bimmi set the cat down and jumped to his feet.

"*Merci*, *merci beaucoup*, ma'am!" he said, almost too happy to speak. "Oh, *merci!* Me, I take such good care of this cat, you never see such! And you need me to help you with things, just ask someone to tell Bimmi Ladouce!"

And Bimmi leaped through the gate and ran down the white oyster-shell road to tell Mama the most exciting thing in the world.

Elisabeth Jane Stewart was born and raised in Galveston, Texas, where she knew a crabber's son who inspired the character of Bimmi in this story. A graduate of East Texas State Teachers College and Northern Arizona University, Ms. Stewart taught children from fifth grade up to junior high for twenty-five years. She now lives in Tucson, Arizona, with her husband and three cats. Her previous book for Clarion was *On the Long Trail Home*.

James E. Ransome was born in North Carolina and moved to New Jersey as a teenager. A graduate of Pratt Institute, he recently completed a mural for the Children's Museum of Indianapolis. He has also illustrated James Weldon Johnson's *The Creation*, winner of the Coretta Scott King Award for Illustration, and—for Clarion—Elizabeth Fitzgerald Howard's *Aunt Flossie's Hats (And Crab Cakes Later)*.

James Ransome lives in upstate New York with his wife, Lesa; their daughters, Jaime and Maya; and their Dalmatian, Clinton.